PUPPIES
Are Like That

A Random House PICTUREBACK®

Puppies Ar

 Published in the United States by Random House, Inc., New York, and simultaneously in Canada by Random House of Canada Limited, Toronto. ISBN: 0-394-82923-9. Library of Congress Catalog Card Number: 74-2542.

Manufactured in the United States of America

19 20

Like That

by Jan Pfloog

Random House New York

Puppies like to chew on things—

like bones,

or rubber balls,

or even sticks.

This puppy is chewing on somebody's sneaker.
He will have to be scolded.

Puppies don't like to be scolded.
They hang their heads and tuck in their tails
and look very sorry.

But a few minutes later
their tails are wagging again.

Puppies are like that!

Puppies think it is great fun to bark.
They will bark at nothing just to see who can bark loudest.

Or they will bark at something that flies, like a butterfly.

When puppies feel very brave, they bark at animals much bigger than they are.

Best of all, they like barking at cats.

Puppies are like that!

But barking at cats can be a big mistake!

Puppies like to play together.
These puppies are playing tug of war
to see which one is stronger.

Puppies think that every dog is their friend.

But some big dogs want to be left alone.

These puppies are having a race to see which one can run faster.

Puppies are like that!

Puppies are curious.

They find all sorts of strange and interesting animals.

Some move surprisingly fast.

Others move very slowly.

This puppy is sniffing in a woodchuck burrow
to see if anyone is at home.

The woodchuck is watching from his back door.

Puppies love to chase things.

They will chase anything that runs or flies— especially rabbits,

or birds,

or squirrels.

But they almost never catch anything.

Puppies like to dig, especially where the dirt is nice and soft, as in a garden.

This makes them very dirty, but they don't care.

Puppies are like that!

When a puppy gets very dirty—
like this one—he must have a bath.

Puppies don't like baths.
They hate to be wet and cold.

But they love to be dried in a warm towel.

Puppies don't always want to run and dig and play.
Sometimes they just want to curl up
in their beds and go to sleep.

Puppies are like that, too!